The Snugglewump

Written by

Lou Treleaven

Illustrated by

Kate Chappell

For Mum and Dad. LT

For Dad and Mum. KC

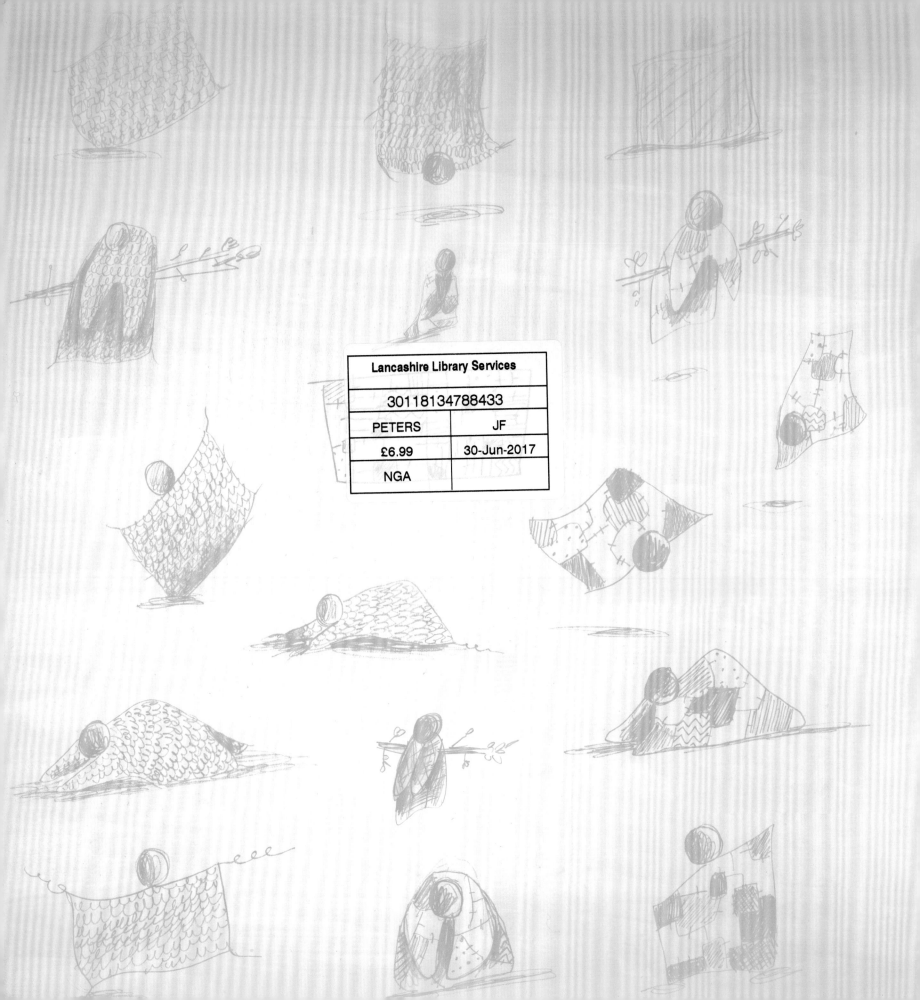

Molly's toys were bored one day, lined up along the bed.

What about me?

She'll soon be home to play with me.
She loves me best," said Ted.

"Excuse me," said an ancient doll,
arising with a creak.
"I think you'll find I'm much admired
- and what's more, I'm antique."

I'm quite old too.

"Look out below!" yelled Action Andy, parachuting past.

"You soppy lot just sit about.
With me she has a blast."

I could be
a parachute.

"You puny Earthlings can't compete," said Alien, oozing by.

"My slimy skin and tentacles make me her favourite guy."

I'm more the soft and squidgy type.

"Illogical," said Robot,
as he beeped and zoomed about.

But just before he could say more, his batteries ran out.

They all forgot the Snugglewump. It listened as it lay.

Then, sighing, flopped on to the floor and snugglewumped away.

It flopped out of the catflap.

Along the street it blew.

For half a mile, it spent a while stuck
to a postman's shoe.

It fell off in a puddle and was kicked into the park.
And there it lay for all that day until the sky grew dark.

"How nice to be a toy," it thought,
"with arms and legs and face.
I'm just a square with nothing there,
an empty waste of space.

How nice to have a battery
and whizz around all day.
I'm just a scrag of tatty rag
 that should be thrown away."

Then as it lay upon the grass,
all cold and wet and manky,
a sniffly rabbit bounded up
and used it as a hanky.

The night passed slowly,
then at last a pink haze filled the sky.

Two pigeons took the Snugglewump
and hung it up to dry.

Molly!

"The time has surely come," it thought.
"I'll soon be in the dump."

But then it heard a voice it knew.
"I've found my Snugglewump!"

As Molly took it in her arms,
it understood quite rightly:

You know how much you're treasured
when your loved one holds you tightly.

The End

The Snugglewump
An original concept by author Lou Treleaven
© Lou Treleaven
Illustrated by Kate Chappell

MAVERICK ARTS PUBLISHING LTD
Studio 3A, City Business Centre, 6 Brighton Road, Horsham, West Sussex, RH13 5BB
© Maverick Arts Publishing Limited May 2017 +44 (0)1403 256941

Published May 2017

A CIP catalogue record for this book is available at the British Library.

ISBN 978-1-84886-241-8

Maverick
arts publishing
www.maverickbooks.co.uk